The Glorious
ABC

Sarah Stillwell, 1904

Harriet Bennett, 1897

The Glorious ABC

Selected by Cooper Edens

with illustrations by the best artists from the past

ATHENEUM   1990   NEW YORK

Biographical information about the
artists and a list of sources of
the illustrations appear at the end
of the book.

Atheneum
Macmillan Publishing Company
866 Third Avenue, New York, NY 10022
Collier Macmillan Canada, Inc.
Designed by Barbara A. Fitzsimmons
First Edition
Printed in Hong Kong
10 9 8 7 6 5 4 3 2 1

Library of Congress Cataloging-in-Publication Data
The Glorious ABC / selected by Cooper Edens.
—1st ed.   p.   cm.
Includes bibliographical references.
Summary: The illustration for each letter is taken from a
book by one of twenty-eight different artists who flourished
between 1874 and 1926. Brief biographies of each illustrator (Boutet
de Monvel, Crane, Willebeek Le Mair, Dulac, Parrish, Brooke,
Rackham, etc.) are included.
ISBN 0-689-31605-4
1. English language—Alphabet—Juvenile literature.
[1. Alphabet.] I. Edens, Cooper.
PE1155.G55 1990 [E]—dc20
90-30566 CIP AC

FOREWORD

Baseball fans never tire of assembling an imaginary team of the greatest players of all time. On this team one can have Lou Gehrig at first base, Honus Wagner at shortstop, Johnny Bench catching, Willie Mays in centerfield, etc., etc. I am a collector of old children's books, and I play the same kind of game with my favorite illustrators. This book presents my team. My favorites are used to illustrate each of the letters, and I hope you will find it as impressive a lineup as I do. My only regret is similar to the baseball fan's who cannot help worrying, "Maybe I should use Walter Johnson as my starting pitcher instead of Sandy Koufax." There are simply too many great players to make a single team, and too many great illustrators to adorn an alphabet book. How, I ask myself, could I not include L. J. Bridgman, or Oliver Herford, or E. V. B., or A. B. Frost, or Kay Nielsen, or Florence Upton? But, just as with my baseball team, what we do have is of superb quality, and I am confident it makes a book that many children will learn from and enjoy. I also hope this collection will awaken in children and their parents a desire to explore and collect from the Hall of Fame of old children's books.

C. E.

Emilie Benson Knipe, 1914

*I dedicate this book to all of the artists who have created beautiful
pictures for children's books, particularly some of my favorite
illustrators for whom I could not find a place in this book:
Ida Waugh, Margaret Ely Webb, Maria Kirk, E.V.B.,
Warwick Goble, Milo Winter, Job, A.L. Bowley,
Graham Robertson, Edward Lear, Mars, L.D. Bradley,
John Lawson, Jennie Harbour, Fanny Cory, and,
most of all, Anonymous, who labored endlessly, fruitfully,
and with little recognition.*

C. E.

The Glorious ABC

A is for Artist

Maurice Boutet de Monvel, 1900

B is for Bubble

Kate Greenaway, 1887

C is for Cat

Louis Wain, 1905

D is for Duck

E. Boyd Smith, 1910

E is for Elephant

Harry Neilson, about 1900

F is for Frog

Walter Crane, 1874

G is for Gingerbread Man

Johnny Gruelle, 1914

H is for Hat

Harriett Bennett, about 1885

I is for Invisible

John R. Neill, 1908

J is for Jumping Rope

Henriette Willebeek Le Mair, 1914

K is for Kiss

Edmund Dulac, 1911

L is for Lanterns

Maxfield Parrish, 1910

M is for Moon

Anne Anderson, about 1915

N is for Night

Ida Rentoul Outhwaite, 1926

O is for Ocean

Margaret W. Tarrant, 1923

P is for Pig

L. Leslie Brooke, 1905

Q is for Queen

Millicent Sowerby, 1908

R is for Rabbit

Beatrix Potter, 1912

S is for Somersault

W. Heath Robinson, 1912

T is for Train

Honor Appleton, 1920

U is for Umbrella

Palmer Cox, 1895

V is for Visit

Randolph Caldecott, 1883

W is for Watermelon

Charles Robinson, 1909

X is for eXercise

Arthur Rackham, 1918

Y is for Youth

Jessie Willcox Smith, 1908

Z is for Zeal

Peter Newell, 1901

ABOUT THE ARTISTS

ANNE ANDERSON was a Scottish artist. She married another artist, Alan Wright, and they sometimes worked together on children's books. Anne enjoyed making picture books for small children. Her pictures show us a world where happy children possess a powerful awareness of the wonder of the world. Some of her works are *The Funny Bunny Book*, *The Cosy Corner Book*, and *Cosy Time Tales*. Anne Anderson was born in 1874.

HONOR APPLETON was an English book illustrator. We know very little about her life, but from her books we can tell that she loved toys and dolls. Almost all of her books were about children playing with their toys, which often come to life. Some of her books are *The Bad Mrs. Ginger*, *Josephine and Her Dolls*, *Josephine's Happy Family*, and *The Best Teddy Bear in the World*. Her style was one of great delicacy. We don't know her birth and death dates, but her books were published from 1902 through 1940.

HARRIET BENNETT was an English painter who exhibited many paintings at The Royal Academy between 1877 and 1892. We know little about her life, except that her pictures were beautifully reproduced in a number of children's books, including *Old Father Time*, *All Around the Clock*, and *A Round Robin*. Her pictures excel in realistic detail.

LOUIS MAURICE BOUTET DE MONVEL was a painter and book illustrator whom the French considered a supreme master at depicting children. Some of his books are *Boys and Girls*, *Our Children*, and *The Book of Manners*. He was born in 1850 and died in 1913.

LEONARD LESLIE BROOKE was an English illustrator who lived from 1862 to 1940. He created many picture books, including *Johnny Crow's Garden*, *The Story of the Three Bears*, *The Golden Goose*, and *Ring o' Roses*. Most of his characters are animals, which he usually depicts standing upright and greatly enjoying life.

RANDOLPH CALDECOTT, one of the best known of all children's book illustrators, loved the English countryside and the lively characteristics and life-styles of the people and animals who lived there. He chose to illustrate old folk stories and rhymes like *Sing a Song for Sixpence*, *Hey Diddle Diddle*, *The House That Jack Built*, and *Bye, Baby Bunting*. His pictures abound in movement, humor, and interesting details. He was born in 1846 and died in 1886, shortly after arriving in the United States.

PALMER COX was Canadian. He illustrated many kinds of books, but became famous for his characters who were known as Brownies. These little people were the subject of book after book, which showed them traveling around the world, creating good-natured mischief everywhere. Some of the titles were *The Brownies at Home*, *The Brownies Around the World*, and *The Brownies: Their Book*. His jam-packed, humorous pictures were enjoyed in almost every home in America. Cox was born in 1840 and died in 1924.

WALTER CRANE, who lived from 1845 to 1915, was a whirlwind of creative energy. He designed wallpaper, cloth, costumes, tiles, and many other things, and was a prolific painter and book illustrator as well. The pictures he made for books were complicated, colorful, and were always clearly the work of Walter Crane. Some of his books were *The House That Jack Built*, *The Frog Prince*, *Jack and the Beanstalk*, and *Old Mother Hubbard*.

EDMUND DULAC was born in France but settled in England when he was a young man. He was active in many areas of art, including costumes for the theater, postage stamps, bank notes, furniture design, and portrait painting. He illustrated many books, including *Tales from the Arabian Knights*, *Stories from Hans Andersen*, and *A Fairy Garland*. Dulac made marvelous pictures that are drawn with great accuracy and detail. He lived from 1882 to 1953.

KATE GREENAWAY was an English artist who liked to make pictures of children in elaborate costumes that were old-fashioned, even in her time. Austin Dobson said of her, "No one has given us such clear-eyed, soft-faced, happy-hearted childhood." A few of her works are *Under the Window*, *A Day in a Child's Life*, and *A Book of Games*. She lived from 1846 to 1901.

JOHNNY GRUELLE was an American illustrator who will forever be remembered as the creator of Raggedy Ann and Andy. These famous cloth dolls are happy and calm through all their incredible adventures. Some of his books are *Raggedy Ann Stories*, *The Paper Dragon*, and *Rhymes for Kindly Children*. Gruelle was born in 1880 and died in 1938.

EMILIE BENSON KNIPE was born in Philadelphia, Pennsylvania, in 1870. She died in 1958. Her husband, Alden Knipe, was an author of children's books, and she illustrated many of his books, including *Boys* and *Girls*.

HENRIETTE WILLEBEEK LE MAIR was born in the Netherlands in 1889 and lived until 1966. Her delicate watercolor paintings almost always show us ideal children in beautiful surroundings. A few of her books are *Old Dutch Nursery Rhymes*, *Little People*, and *The Children's Corner*.

JOHN R. NEILL was an American artist who illustrated thirty-five books about the Land of Oz. Neill's imagination was as rich as L. Frank Baum's, the author of the Oz books, and together they made this fantastic land real and memorable. Oz was further made popular by the movie *The Wizard of Oz*. A few of the books Neill illustrated are *The Marvelous Land of Oz*, *Ozma of Oz*, *The Road to Oz*, and *The Tin Woodman of Oz*. He was born in 1876 and died in 1943.

HARRY NEILSON, an Englishman, created many books in which animals acted like human beings. His pictures were humorous and energetic. Some of the titles are *The Animals' Academy*, *Christmas at the Zoo*, and *Jumbo Tales*. He was born in 1861 and died in 1941.

PETER NEWELL was an American artist who liked best to create children's books. He was very imaginative and wrote almost all of his books as well as illustrated them. His people and animals are instantly recognizable as his creations, for they brim with a frenzied energy. Some of his works are *Topsys and Turveys*, *The Hole Book*, *The Slant Book*, and *The Rocket Book*. He was born in 1862 and died in 1924.

IDA RENTOUL OUTHWAITE was a self-taught artist. She was the first Australian children's book illustrator to achieve world fame. She loved to paint fairies and other magical people. In her pictures they often played with kangaroos, koalas, and other Australian animals. She was born in 1888 and died in 1960.

MAXFIELD PARRISH was an American artist who was taught art by his father. He made many murals for public buildings, painted pictures for calendars, and illustrated a variety of books. His strong colors and the way he used light in his paintings made him very popular. Some of his books are *The Knave of Hearts*, *The Arabian Knights*, *Dream Days*, and *Poems of Childhood*. He painted until he was ninety-one years old. He was born in 1870 and died in 1966.

BEATRIX POTTER was English. When she was a little girl she had few human friends and spent much of her time with animals. She practiced painting and drawing pictures of her animal friends and became one of the finest wildlife artists of her time. When she was twenty-nine years old she wrote a series of letters to a sick young friend telling the friend about a rabbit. These developed into *The Tale of Peter Rabbit*, which was so popular that she wrote and illustrated more than twenty little books over the next thirty years. Some of them were *The Tailor of Gloucester*, *The Tale of Two Bad Mice*, and *The Pie and the Patty Pan*. She lived from 1864 to 1943.

ARTHUR RACKHAM was the most admired British illustrator of his time. He illustrated many of the classics of children's literature, and brought to each the skills of a fine painter and a powerful belief in the reality of each book's characters. Some of his books were *Peter Pan*, *The Pied Piper*, *A Christmas Carol*, and *The Wind in the Willows*. He lived from 1867 to 1939.

CHARLES ROBINSON was the son of an English illustrator, and the brother of two other creators of books, Thomas Heath Robinson and William Heath Robinson, whose illustration accompanies the letter "S" in this volume. Charles was very prolific but had two principal styles—one childishly simple and the other exquisitely complex. Some of his books are *The Silly Submarine*, *Animals in Wrong Places*, *Peculiar Piggies*, and *The Cake Shop*. He was born in 1870 and died in 1937.

WILLIAM HEATH ROBINSON was a British artist who was born into a family of book illustrators. His brother Charles's work appears in this volume under the letter "W." William was skillful at many kinds of illustration, but he gained his fame principally for his humorous pictures. He was born in 1872 and died in 1944. Some of his books are *The Adventures of Uncle Lubin*, *Absurdities*, *How to Make a Garden Grow*, and *Peacock Pie*.

E. BOYD SMITH was a Canadian who came to live in the United States and did most of his work here. He had the twin gifts of capturing reality and seeing the humor in the world around him. *The Story of Noah's Ark*, *Santa Claus and All About Him*, and *Chicken World* are three of his most popular books. He was born in 1863 and lived until 1943.

JESSIE WILLCOX SMITH was an American artist who studied under the great illustrator and teacher Howard Pyle. She was a kindergarten teacher, but because of bad health, turned to illustration to make a living. She developed a great skill at portraying young people and in many magazine covers and books revealed her insights into the moods and dreams of childhood. Some of her books are *Dream Blocks*, *Rhymes of Real Children*, *The Everyday Fairy Book*, and *The Seven Ages of Childhood*. She was born in 1863 and died in 1935.

AMY MILLICENT SOWERBY was born in 1878, the daughter of an artistically gifted English family. With her sister Githa she collaborated on many books, including *Bumbletoes*, *The Pretty Book*, *Yesterday's Children*, and *The Happy Book*. She said of her work: "Being very fond of children, I turned naturally to painting them and for them. It has always been the beautiful in childhood that has attracted me...I love flowers and bright colors." She died in 1967.

SARAH STILLWELL, an American illustrator, was born in 1878 and died in 1939. Like Jessie Willcox Smith (above), she studied for many years under Howard Pyle. The inner life of the child was her favorite subject. Two of her books are *Childhood* and *The Luxury of Children*.

MARGARET W. TARRANT was an English artist who for fifty years created art for posters, greeting cards, calendars, postcards, and books. The grace and simplicity of her work made her enormously popular, particularly during the 1920s and 1930s. A few of her books were *Verses for Children*, *The Book of Games*, *The Water Babies*, and *Nursery Rhymes*. She lived from 1888 to 1959.

LOUIS WAIN was an English illustrator who published, in books and magazines, more than five hundred pictures a year and created at that rate for many years. He was very fond of animals and was a leader in several organizations that encouraged kindness to animals. Cats were his favorite subject. Some of his books were *Kittenland*, *The Cat Scouts*, and *Fun and Frolic*. He lived from 1860 to 1939.

SOURCES OF ILLUSTRATIONS

Half title   from *Rhymes and Jingles*. Gay and Bird, 1904.

Frontispiece   Lang, Andrew, editor. *The Nursery Rhyme Book*. Frederick Warne and Co., 1897.

Second half title   from *A Child's Christmas*. Blackie and Son Limited, 1906.

Foreword   from *Remember Rhymes*. Hearst International Library, 1914.

A   from France, Anatole. *Filles et Garçons*. Librarie Hachette, 1900.

B   from Allingham, William. *Rhymes for the Young Folk*. Cassell and Co., 1887.

C   from *The Louis Wain Annual*. Raphael Tuck and Sons Ltd., 1905.

D   from *Chicken World*. G.P. Putnam's Sons, 1910.

E   from Bird, Cockiolly. *Droll Doings*. Blackie and Son Limited, 1905.

F   from *The Frog Prince*. George Routledge and Sons, 1874.

G   from *My Very Own Fairy Stories*. P.F. Volland Company, 1914.

H   from Mack, Robert Ellice. *Queen of the Meadow*. E.P. Dutton and Company, about 1885.

I   from Baum, L. Frank. *Dorothy and the Wizard In Oz*. The Reilly and Britton Co., 1908.

J   from Elkin, R.H. *The Children's Corner*. David McKay, 1914.

K   from *Stories from Hans Andersen*. Hodder and Stoughton, 1911.

L   from "Collier's," 1910.

M   from *The Little Busy Bee Book*. Thomas Nelson and Sons, about 1915.

N   from Rentoul, Annie R., and Outhwaite, Grenbry. *Fairyland*. Frederick A. Stokes Company, 1926.

O   from St. John-Webb, Marion. *The Littlest One*. George G. Harrap and Co. Ltd., 1923.

P   from *The Golden Goose Book*. Frederick Warne and Co. Ltd., 1905.

Q   from Sowerby, Githa. *Yesterday's Children*. Chatto and Windus, 1908.

R   from *The Tale of Mr. Tod*. Frederick Warne and Co., 1912.

S   from *Bill the Minder*. George H. Doran Co., 1912.

T   from Craddock, Mrs. H.C. *Josephine Goes Travelling*. Blackie and Son Limited, 1920.

U   from *Brownie Yearbook*. McLoughlin Bro's., 1895.

V   from *The Hey Diddle Diddle Picture Book*. Frederick Warne and Co. Ltd., 1883.

W   from Pope, Jessie. *Babes and Birds*. H.M. Caldwell Company, 1909.

X   from Swinburne, Algernon Charles. *The Springtide of Life*. J.B. Lippincott Company, 1918.

Y   from Higgins, Aileen Cleveland. *Dream Blocks*. Duffield and Company, 1908.

Z   from Wells, Carolyn. *Mother Goose's Menagerie*. Noyes, Platt, and Company, 1901.